Rupa

Raises

the

Sun

by Marsha Wilson Chall

with illustrations by
Rosanne Litzinger

A DK INK BOOK
DK PUBLISHING, INC.

To R.W.J.: She finally saw the light.
—M.W.C.

To Roger

Best wishes.
—R.L.

A *Richard Jackson* Book

DK Publishing, Inc., 95 Madison Avenue, New York, New York 10016
Visit us on the World Wide Web at http://www.dk.com

Library of Congress Cataloging-in-Publication Data
Chall, Marsha Wilson.
Rupa raises the sun / by Marsha Wilson Chall; illustrated by Rosanne Litzinger.—1st ed.
p. cm. "A Richard Jackson Book"
Summary: Every dark and cold morning Rupa tromps around her tiny cookfire in order to raise the sun,
but when she decides it is time for a rest the village elders must try to find a substitute.
ISBN 0-7894-2496-7 [1. Sun—Rising and setting—Fiction.] I. Litzinger, Rosanne, ill. II. Title.
PZ7.C3494Ru 1998 [Fic]—dc21 97-47294 CIP AC

The illustrations for this book were painted using opaque watercolor (gouache)
applied very carefully to Mr. Arches 140 lb. cold pressed watercolor paper.
The text of this book is set in 18 point Quorum Book. Printed and bound in U.S.A.
First Edition, 1998
10 9 8 7 6 5 4 3 2 1

Stoddart
Kids

Published in Canada in 1998 by Stoddart Kids, a division of Stoddart
Publishing Co. Limited, 34 Lesmill Road, Toronto, Canada M3B 2T6

Distributed in Canada by General Distribution Services,
30 Lesmill Road, Toronto, Canada M3B 2T6

Tel (416) 445-3333   Fax (416) 445-5967
E-mail Customer.Service@ccmailgw.genpub.com

Canadian Cataloguing in Publication Data
Chall, Marsha Wilson Rupa Raises the sun
ISBN 0-7737-3109-1

It happened long ago,
and it wouldn't be told
if it hadn't, that old Rupa
got up early every morning
to raise the sun. Even Rupa
wondered how she did it.
Still, each morning as she
tromped around her cookfire,
the sun broke across the sky
like an egg yolk.
"Eureka!" Rupa
always yelled then.
"Ki-ki-ri-ki!" her rooster
always crowed.

Every dark morning, every dark
and cold morning, old Rupa
raised the sun before the baker,
the blacksmith, and baby Tekla
were awake. After all, if she didn't,
who would? They were asleep
in their warm straw beds.
Most winter mornings, Rupa
wished she were, too,
especially one morning
when she woke with a great
blister on her foot
and greater frost on her mustache.
"Ugh," she said, and raised
the sun. But as soon as she'd
done the job, she hobbled into
the village where the elders
were taking their morning tea.

"I've had enough," she told them. "Twenty-one thousand nine hundred fifty-four sun-ups, and now this!" She plopped her foot onto the elders' table. They covered their breakfast plates.

"I need a vacation," Rupa said.
"Rupa," said the eldest elder. "Please
remember that the sun must rise
to warm the days and thaw our bones."
"Then I need a substitute for
a few mornings," she said.
"Hmmm," said the elders.
"We'll have to think about that."
So Rupa sat down on the floor to wait.
The elders put their heads together.
At last the eldest elder spoke.
"We'll hold sun-raising tryouts
tonight at Rupa's."
"Sensible idea," said Rupa,
and she lumbered home.

The night sky hung thick
as a carpet over Rupa's hut.
The villagers tried in turn
to raise the sun.
First the blacksmith.
"I make flames as hot as
the sun and higher than Rupa,
who calls the sun each day
with her tiny cookfire. If she
can do it, then surely so can I."
And he hammered eight
glowing cartwheels in his forge,
but night merely deepened,
black as his thumbnails.

The goat farmer came next.
"Rupa's rooster welcomes
the sun each morning.
My goats give milk then, too.
I will milk them to greet the sun."
He squatted, tugged and squeezed,
whispered, "Isabella, if you please."
But she didn't. Hortense couldn't.
Camilla wouldn't. No sun,
no milk.

Then the baker tried. "Rupa
always cooks breakfast over her fire.
Surely I can invite the sun
to breakfast with my loaves
of warm bread."
The villagers ate all seventy-two loaves
in the dark.

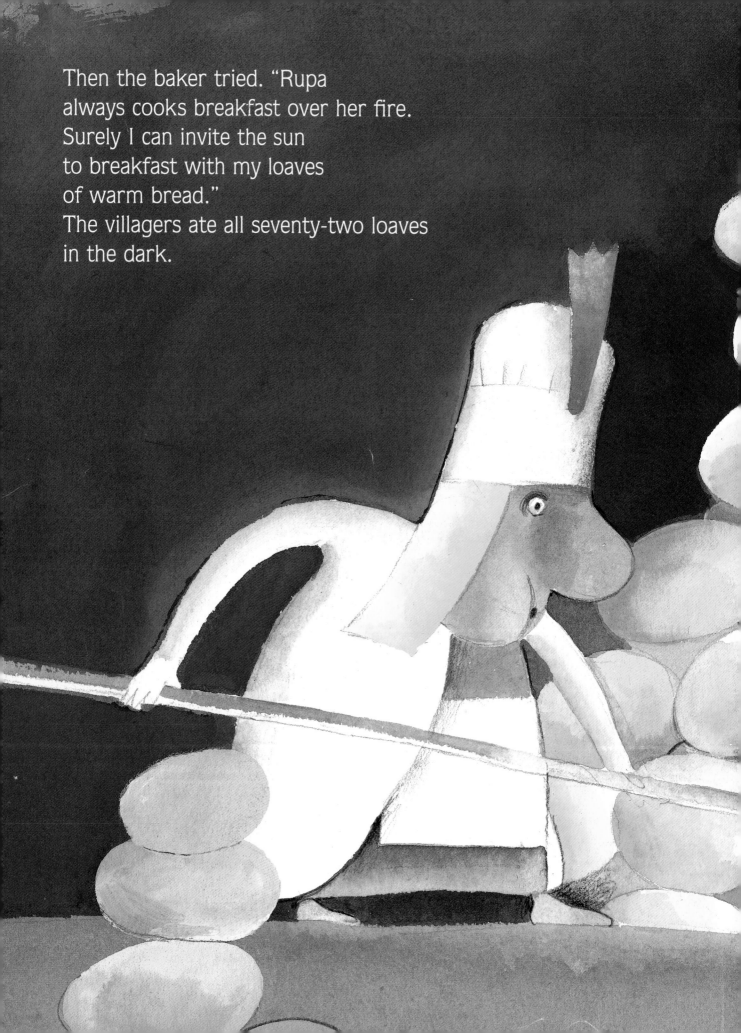

The elders yawned.
"This is taking all night."
And it did.

Everyone fell asleep except Rupa.
"Wake up!" she yelled finally.
"I'll show you how."

She tromped around the fire.
The sun pushed above the hut tops.
"Aaah," the elders sighed.
"Ki-ki-ri-ki!" the rooster crowed.
"Such a gift," said the eldest
elder. "Only you, Rupa."
And he turned to the townspeople.
"I proclaim this 'No Hat Day'
as we remove our hats, caps, and
scarves to honor Rupa."
"Eureka!" the villagers shouted,
and tossed their caps of every color
to the sky.

Again the next morning, Rupa
raised the sun. Slowly. Wearily.
She lifted the bags under her eyes
and trudged to town.
"Rupa, you look awful!"
said the middle elder.
"Now, about that vacation.
You won't have to raise the sun
if you don't let it go down."
"Of course!" said Rupa. "I should
have thought of that."
"Not to worry," said the elder.
"We think for those who don't."

After supper the elders crouched around Rupa's cookfire. The sun settled over the olive trees. "It's time, Rupa," said the middle elder. "Stop the sun from setting." "How?" she asked. "Walk backward around the fire," he answered. Rupa did.

But the sun slipped lower and
lower still.
"You'll have to walk faster,"
the elders told her.
Rupa's blister wouldn't have it.
"This will take all day,"
said the elders. But by then
it was night.

Rupa pointed to her big toe.
"Oh, yes," said the middle elder.
"You must get off your feet."
They put Rupa to bed
and their heads together.
Late that night, the youngest
elder finally spoke.
"Rupa, at least sleep in late
tomorrow. The sun won't rise
on time, but we could all use
the extra rest."

As usual, Rupa woke once again
in the dark. But her blister still
oozed, and the cold floor
reminded her: *sleep in late*.
For the very first time,
Rupa went back to bed.
Yet the more she tried to sleep,
the more she wondered.
If she didn't raise the sun,
how would the rooster crow,
the goats give milk,
the beans sprout?

And as she
wondered, a thin
light spilled in the east,
spread beyond the rim of
night, and dazzled the early sky.
"Ki-ki-ri-ki!" the rooster crowed.
Rupa whispered, "Eureka" as the world
dawned on her. The sun had risen today
on its own. And though Rupa wondered how,
she was grateful. *"Gracias, sol!"*
she cried, and settled back into bed.
The sun simply beamed.

From that day on,
things were the same.
Yet they were different.
At sunrise, the rooster still crowed,
"Ki-ki-ri-ki!"
The goats gave milk.
The beans began to sprout.
The elders took their morning tea.

But Rupa slept in late.